BARNYARD BANTER

FOR LAURA GODWIN,
MY BANTERING BUDDY

SQUARE
FISH
An Imprint of Macmillan

BARNYARD BANTER. Copyright © 1994 by Denise Fleming. All rights reserved.
Printed in China by RR Donnelley Asia Printing Solutions Ltd., Dongguan City,
Guangdong Province.
For information, address Square Fish, 175 Fifth Avenue, New York, NY 10010.

Square Fish and the Square Fish logo are trademarks of Macmillan and
are used by Henry Holt and Company under license from Macmillan.

Library of Congress Cataloging-in-Publication Data
Fleming, Denise.
Barnyard banter / Denise Fleming.
p.   cm.
Summary: All the farm animals are where they should be, clucking and mucking,
mewing and cooing, except for the missing goose.
ISBN 978-0-8050-5581-8
[1. Domestic animals—Fiction. 2. Animal sounds—Fiction. 3. Stories in rhyme.] I. Title.
PZ8.3.F6378Bar 1994   [E]—dc20   93-11032

Originally published in the United States by Henry Holt and Company
First Square Fish Edition: August 2012
Square Fish logo designed by Filomena Tuosto
The illustrations for this book were created with handmade paper.
mackids.com

30

AR: 2.3

BARNYARD BANTER

Denise Fleming

SQUARE • **Henry Holt and Company** • **New York**

Cows in the pasture,
moo,
moo,
moo

Roosters in the barnyard,

cock-a-doodle-doo

Hens in the henhouse,

cluck,

cluck,

cluck

Pigs in the wallow,

muck,

muck,

muck

But where's Goose?

Kittens in the hayloft,

Pigeons
in the rafters,

COO, COO, COO

Mice
in the grain bin,

squeak, squeak,

Peacocks in the wire pen,

shriek,

shriek,

shriek

But where's Goose?

Donkeys in the paddock,

Crows
in the cornfield,

caw,

caw,

caw

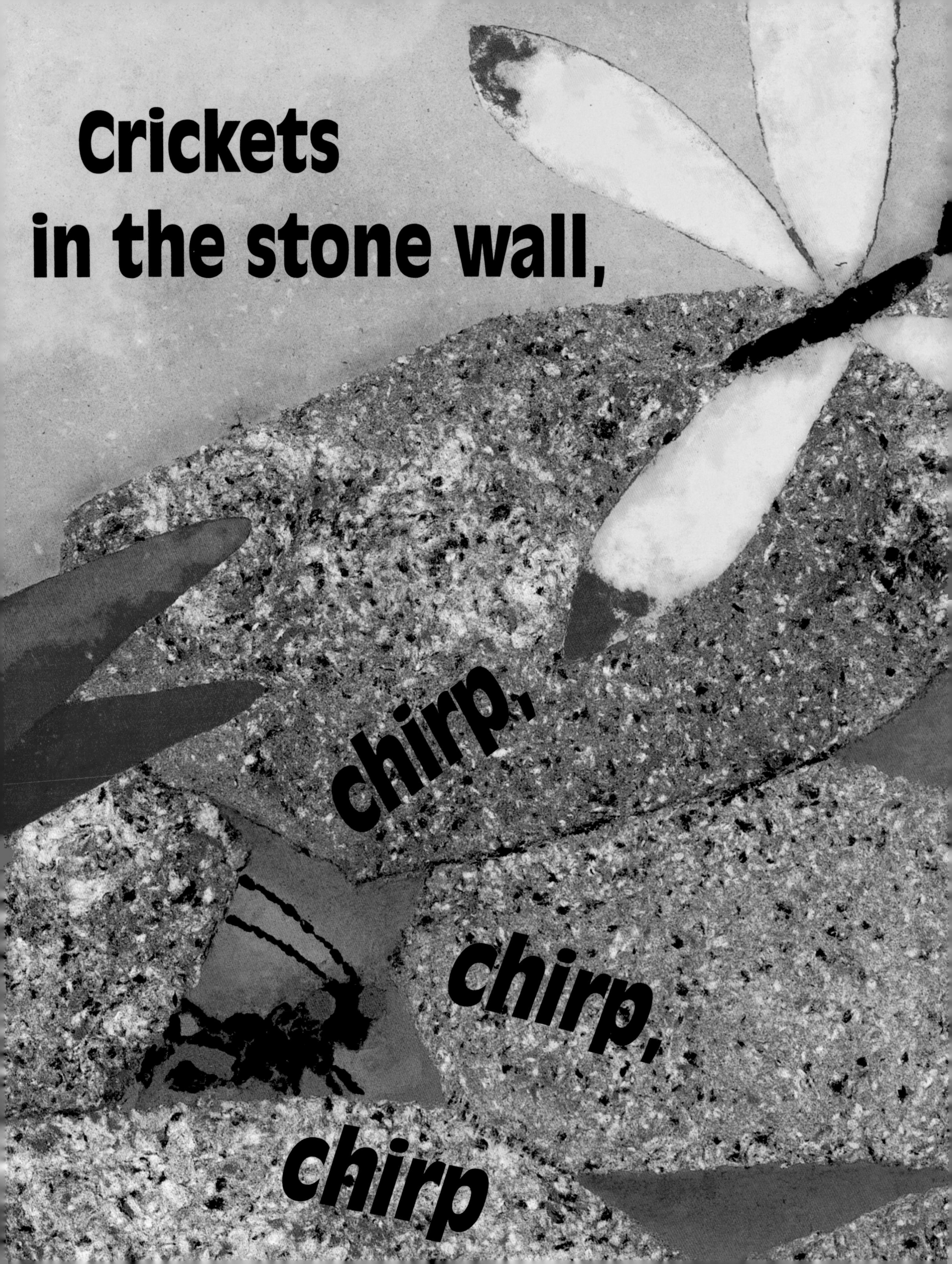

Crickets
in the stone wall,

chirp,

chirp,

chirp

Frogs
in the farm pond,

burp,

burp,

burp

But where's Goose?

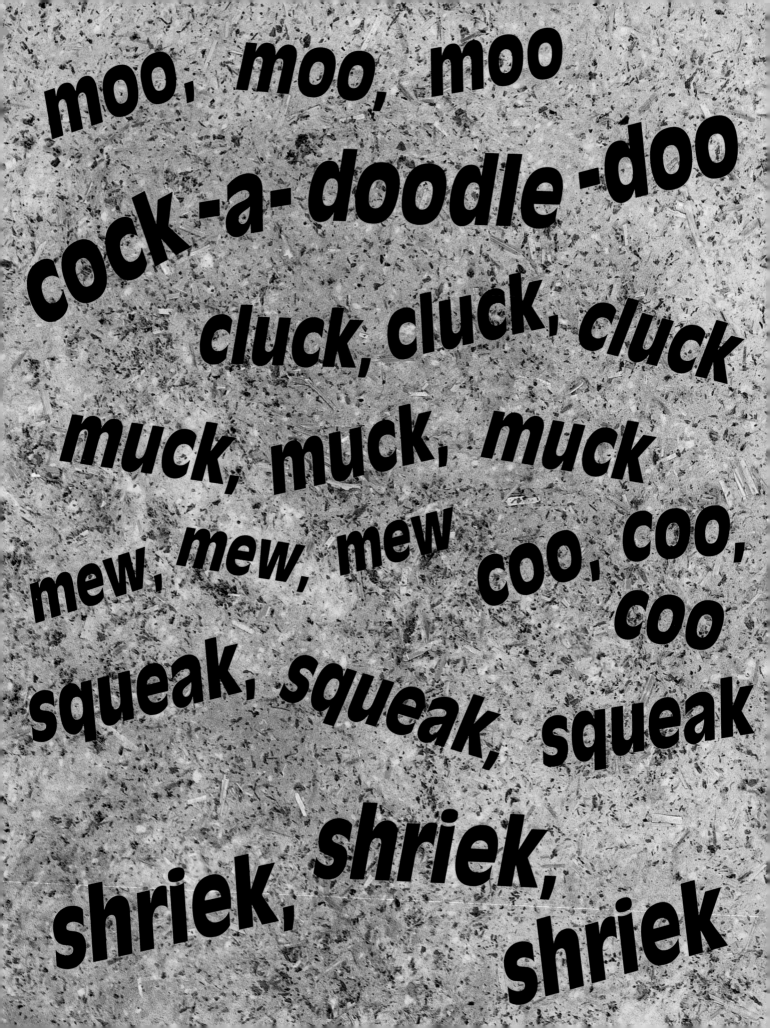

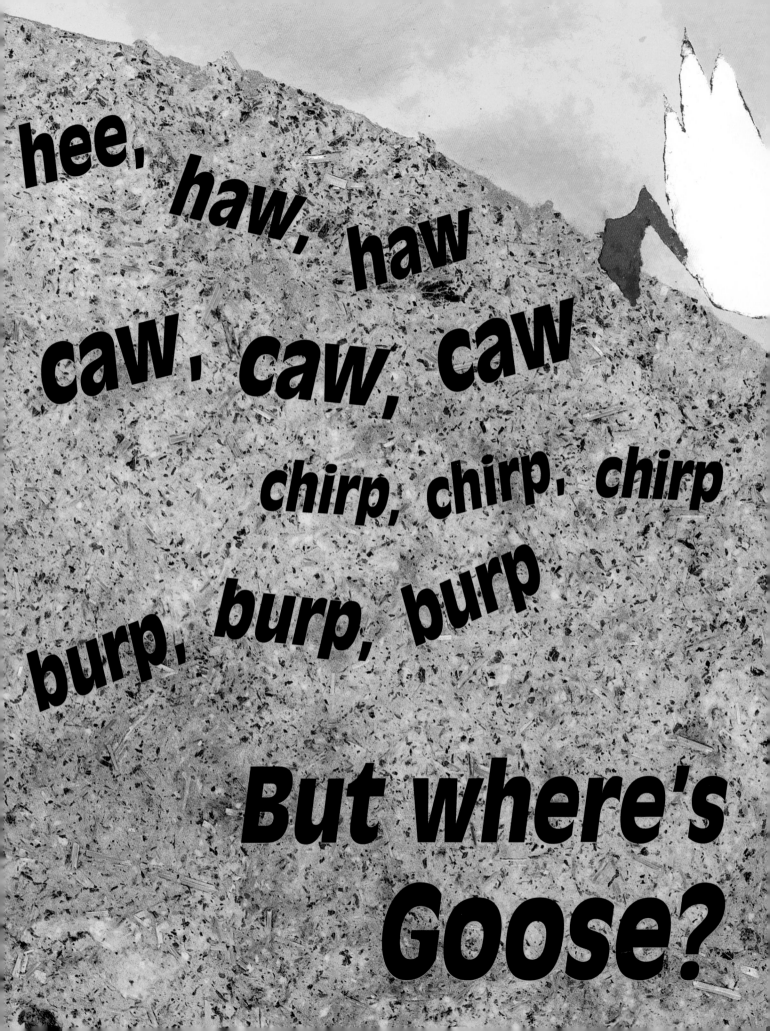

There's Goose!